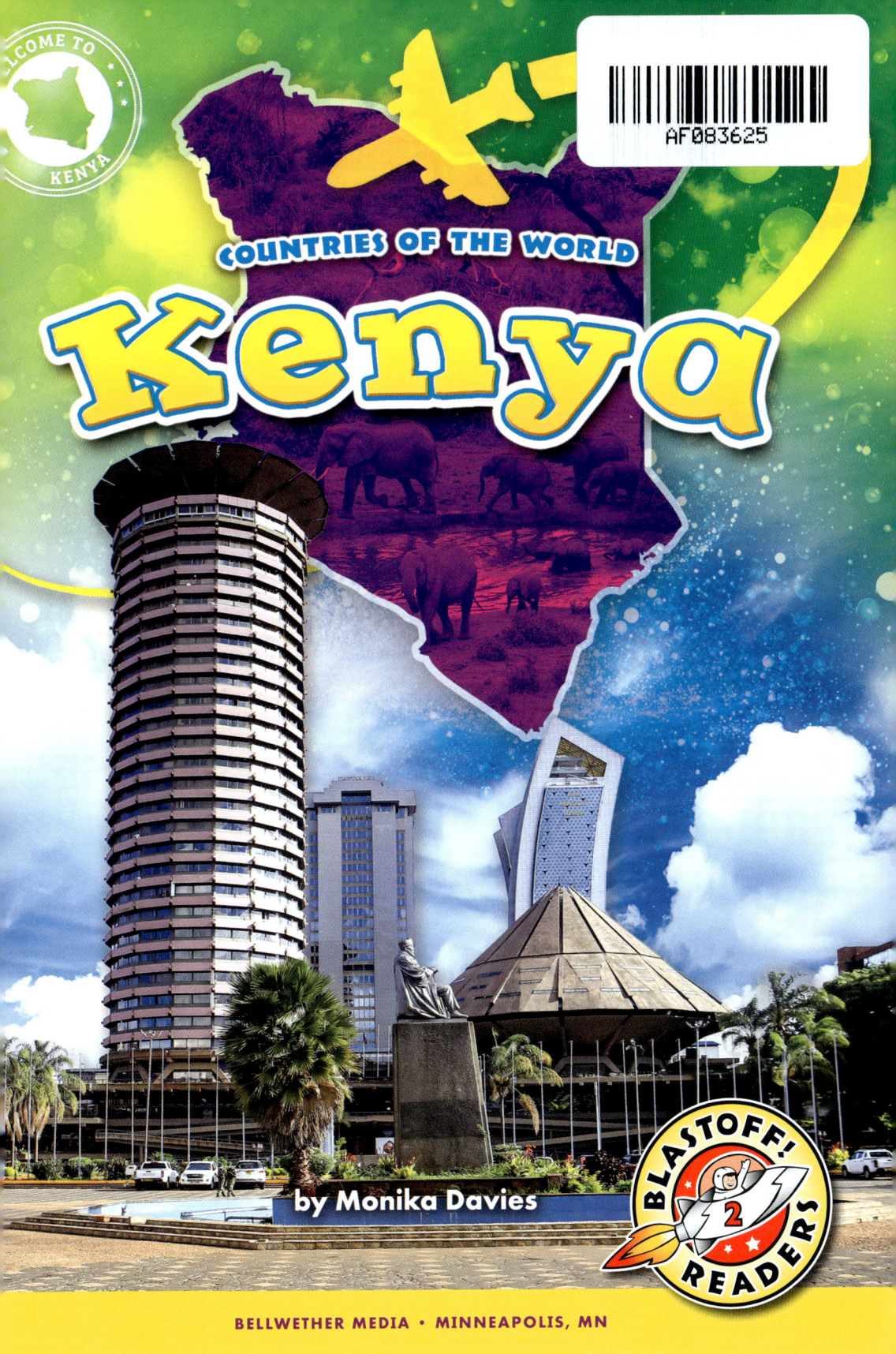

Blastoff! Readers are carefully developed by literacy experts to build reading stamina and move students toward fluency by combining standards-based content with developmentally appropriate text.

 **Level 1** provides the most support through repetition of high-frequency words, light text, predictable sentence patterns, and strong visual support.

 **Level 2** offers early readers a bit more challenge through varied sentences, increased text load, and text-supportive special features.

 **Level 3** advances early-fluent readers toward fluency through increased text load, less reliance on photos, advancing concepts, longer sentences, and more complex special features.

★ **Blastoff! Universe**

Reading Level

This edition first published in 2023 by Bellwether Media, Inc.

No part of this publication may be reproduced in whole or in part without written permission of the publisher. For information regarding permission, write to Bellwether Media, Inc., Attention: Permissions Department, 6012 Blue Circle Drive, Minnetonka, MN 55343.

Library of Congress Cataloging-in-Publication Data

Names: Davies, Monika, author.
Title: Kenya / by Monika Davies.
Other titles: Blastoff! readers. 2, Countries of the world.
Description: Minneapolis : Bellwether Media, Inc., 2023. | Series: Blastoff! Readers. Countries of the world | Includes bibliographical references and index. | Audience: Ages 5-8 | Audience: Grades 2-3 | Summary: "Relevant images match informative text in this introduction to Kenya. Intended for students in kindergarten through third grade"--Provided by publisher.
Identifiers: LCCN 2022044250 (print) | LCCN 2022044251 (ebook) | ISBN 9798886871340 (library binding) | ISBN 9798886872606 (ebook)
Subjects: LCSH: Kenya--Juvenile literature.
Classification: LCC DT433.522 .D38 2023 (print) | LCC DT433.522 (ebook) | DDC 967.62--dc23/eng/20220913
LC record available at https://lccn.loc.gov/2022044250
LC ebook record available at https://lccn.loc.gov/2022044251

Text copyright © 2023 by Bellwether Media, Inc. BLASTOFF! READERS and associated logos are trademarks and/or registered trademarks of Bellwether Media, Inc.

Editor: Elizabeth Neuenfeldt   Designer: Gabriel Hilger

Printed in the United States of America, North Mankato, MN.

Table of Contents

All About Kenya	4
Land and Animals	6
Life in Kenya	12
Kenya Facts	20
Glossary	22
To Learn More	23
Index	24

All About Kenya

Nairobi

Kenya is in East Africa.
It is by the Indian Ocean.
The country's capital is Nairobi.

Kenya has many **reserves**. They are home to **unique** wildlife!

Land and Animals

Savannas cover eastern Kenya. Further west are the highlands.

Deserts lie to the north. Mount Kenya stands tall in the center.

savanna

Mount Kenya

Size: 17,057 feet (5,199 meters) tall

Famous For:

second-tallest mountain in Africa

Northern Kenya is hot and dry. It is **humid** near the coast.

The highlands are cooler.
This area gets the most rain, too.
Many farmers grow crops there.

highlands

Many animals call Kenya home. Elephants roam the highlands. Leopards hunt there, too.

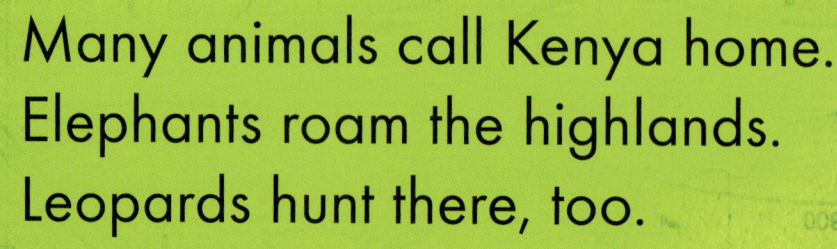

African savanna elephants

Animals of Kenya

leopard

hippo

Nile crocodile

lesser flamingo

Hippos and crocodiles live in rivers. Lesser flamingos **flock** around lakes.

Life in Kenya

Kenyans come from many backgrounds. Most speak English or Swahili.

Many people live in the countryside. But cities are growing. Nairobi is the largest city.

Nairobi

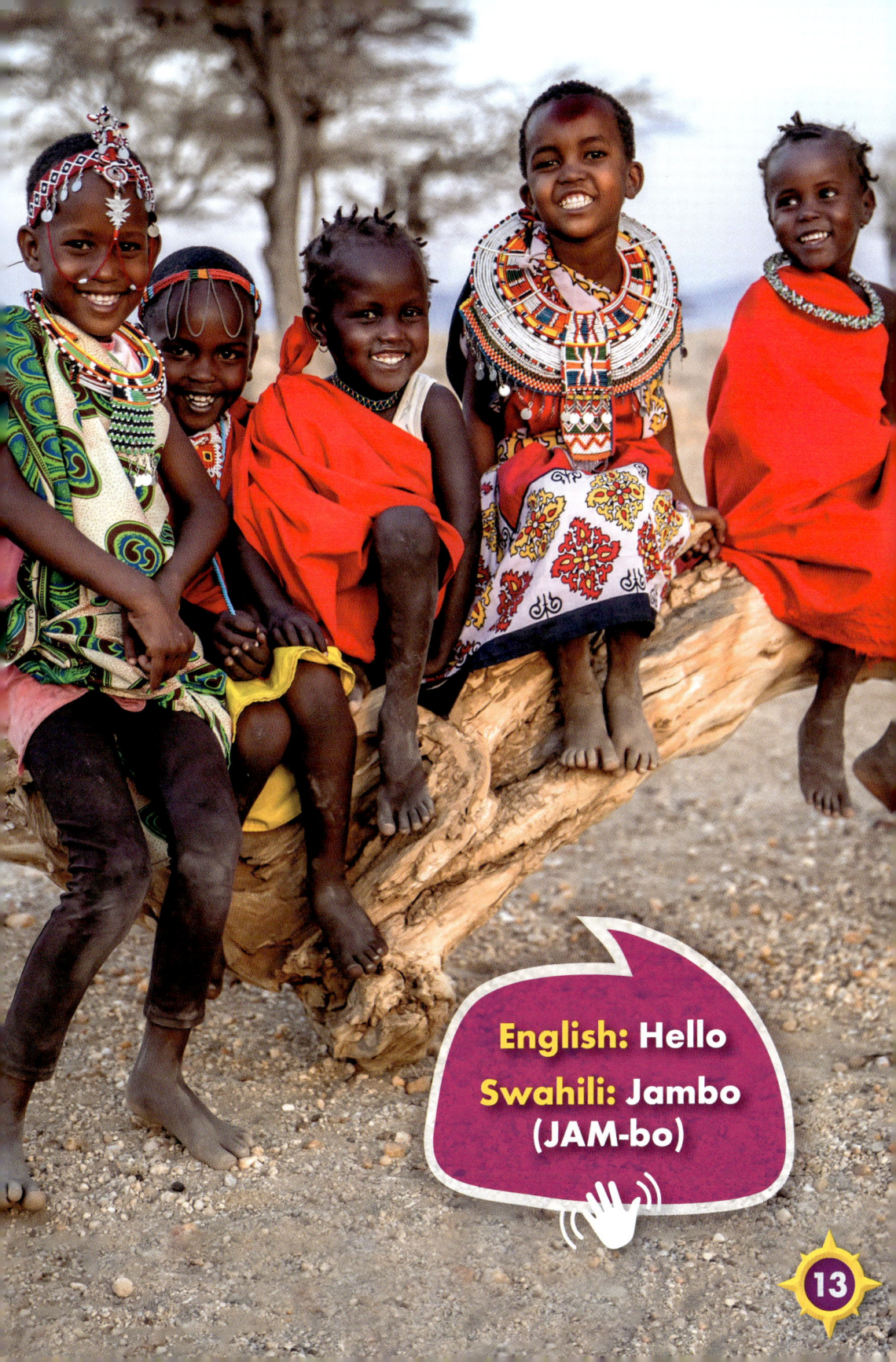

soccer

volleyball

Kenyans enjoy many activities. Some love soccer and volleyball. Many women enjoy **netball**.

Kenyans love to share music and stories. Their songs and stories tell their history.

Ugali is a popular Kenyan food. It is cornmeal porridge eaten with vegetables. *Sukuma wiki* has collard greens.

Kenyan Foods

ugali

sukuma wiki

irio

mandazi

Irio is made of potatoes, corn, and peas. *Mandazi* are sweet donuts.

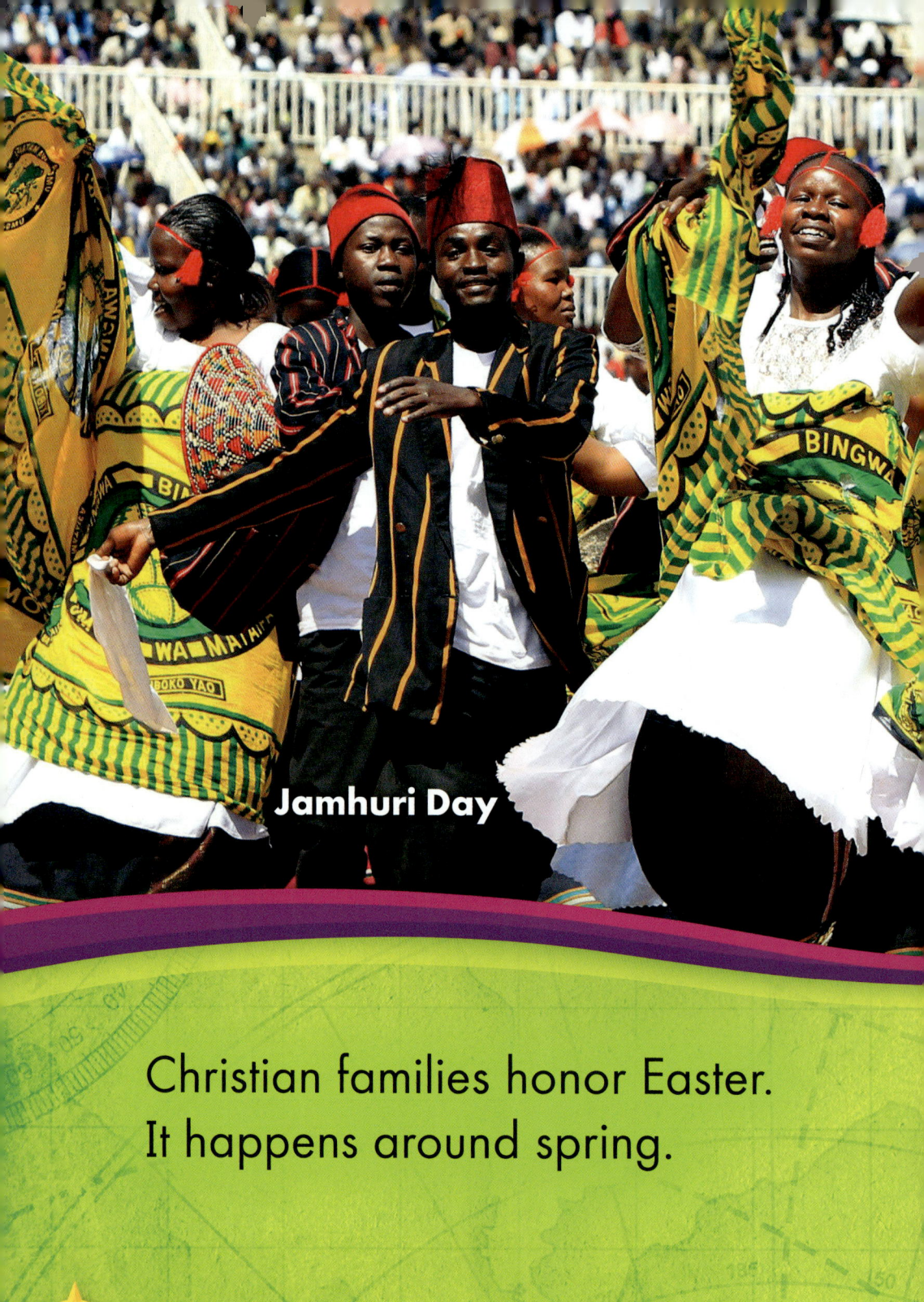

Jamhuri Day

Christian families honor Easter. It happens around spring.

December 12 is Jamhuri Day.
Kenyans sing and dance.
Some **bungee jump** off bridges.
Kenya's national holiday is full of joy!

Kenya Facts

Size:
224,081 square miles
(580,367 square kilometers)

Population:
55,864,655 (2022)

National Holiday:
Jamhuri Day (December 12)

Main Languages:
English, Swahili

Capital City:
Nairobi

Famous Face

Name: Catherine Ndereba

Famous For: a marathon runner known for winning the Boston Marathon four times and winning two Olympic silver medals

Religions

- other 2%
- none 2%
- Muslim 11%
- Christian 85%

Top Landmarks

Bomas of Kenya

Mount Kenya

Tsavo East National Park

Glossary

bungee jump—to jump from a high place while attached to a long, strong rope that stretches and stops you from hitting the ground

deserts—dry lands with few plants and little rainfall

flock—to gather or move around in a crowd

humid—having a lot of water in the air

netball—a sport similar to basketball that has two teams with seven players each

reserves—lands set aside to be protected

savannas—large, flat areas of land with grass and very few trees often found in Africa and South America

unique—very unusual

To Learn More

AT THE LIBRARY

Joubert, Beverly, and Dereck Joubert. *The Ultimate Book of African Animals*. Washington, D.C.: National Geographic Kids, 2021.

Murray, Julie. *Kenya*. Edina, Minn.: Abdo Kids, 2022.

Parkes, Elle. *Let's Explore Kenya*. Minneapolis, Minn.: Lerner Publications, 2018.

ON THE WEB

FACTSURFER

Factsurfer.com gives you a safe, fun way to find more information.

1. Go to www.factsurfer.com.
2. Enter "Kenya" into the search box and click .
3. Select your book cover to see a list of related content.

Index

Africa, 4
animals, 5, 10, 11
capital (see Nairobi)
cities, 12
coast, 8
deserts, 6
Easter, 18
English, 12, 13
food, 16, 17
highlands, 6, 9, 10
Indian Ocean, 4
Jahmuri Day, 18, 19
Kenya facts, 20-21
map, 5
Mount Kenya, 6, 7
music, 15
Nairobi, 4, 5, 12
netball, 14

people, 12
rain, 9
savannas, 6
say hello, 13
soccer, 14
stories, 15
Swahili, 12, 13
volleyball, 14

The images in this book are reproduced through the courtesy of: SOPA Images/ Contributor/ Getty Images, cover; christophe_cerisier, cover; JetKat, p. 3; Sopotnicki, pp. 4-5, 16 (*ugali*), 21 (Bomas of Kenya); Rixpix, p. 6; WanderingNomad, pp. 6-7; Adriana Mahdalova, pp. 8-9; Jen Watson, p. 9; adogslifephoto, pp. 10-11; Hedrus, p. 11 (leopard); Henk Bogaard, p. 11 (hippo); Marius Dobilas, p. 11 (Nile crocodile); Luca Nichetti, p.11 (lesser flamingo); Authentic travel, p. 12; hadnyah, pp. 12-13, 14-15; Andrzej Kubik, p. 14 (inset); Dr Ajay Kumar Singh, p. 15; Fanfo, p. 16 (*sukuma wiki*, *irio*); Sergii Koval, p. 16 (*mandazi*); PreciousPhotos, p. 17; REUTERS/ Alamy, pp. 18-19; titoOnz, p. 20 (flag); The Asahi Shimbun/ Contributor/ Getty Images, p. 20 (Catherine Ndereba); Salparadis, p. 21 (Mount Kenya); Maciej Czekajewski, p. 21 (Tsavo East National Park); Chedko, p. 22.